Edward Arber, Clement Robinson

A Handful of Pleasant Delights

Containing Sundry New Sonnets and Delectable Histories ...

Edward Arber, Clement Robinson

A Handful of Pleasant Delights
Containing Sundry New Sonnets and Delectable Histories ...

ISBN/EAN: 9783337010140

Printed in Europe, USA, Canada, Australia, Japan

Cover: Foto ©Andreas Hilbeck / pixelio.de

More available books at **www.hansebooks.com**

The English Scholar's Library etc.

No. 3.

A Handful of Pleasant Delights, &c.

1584.

The English Scholar's Library of Old and Modern Works.

CLEMENT ROBINSON

and divers others.

A Handful of Pleasant Delights,

Containing sundry new Sonnets and delectable Histories in divers kinds

of metre &c.

1584.

Edited by EDWARD ARBER, F.S.A., etc.,

LECTURER IN ENGLISH LITERATURE ETC.,
UNIVERSITY COLLEGE, LONDON.

SOUTHGATE, LONDON, N.

15 August 1878.

No. 3.

CONTENTS.

A Handefull of pleasant delites, etc. 1

SONGS BEARING THE NAMES OF THEIR AUTHORS.

FIRST LINES OF POEMS & STANZAS.

THE TUNES.

DANCE TUNES.

TUNES CHIEFLY NAMED FROM OLDER BALLADS.

In the Stationers' *Registers*, the first Edition of this *Handful, &c.*, is registered at i. 363.
The Register between 1571–1576 has long been lost. So that the originally Third *Register* is Volume ii. of the *Transcript*. The pages of the references to the various tunes in the *Transcript* will show their relation in time to the first edition of the *Handful, &c.*

BIBLIOGRAPHY.

The three following works will afford help in respect to this Text—

The Ballad Literature and Popular Music of the Olden Time &c. By W. CHAPPELL, F.S.A. 2 Vols. [1855–59] 8vo. [*For the tunes especially.*]

Philobiblon Society. Ancient Ballads and Broadsides published in England in the Sixteenth Century, chiefly in the earlier years of the reign of Queen ELIZABETH. Reprinted from the unique original copies, mostly in Black Letter, preserved in the Library of HENRY HUTH, Esq. London, 1867.

A Transcript of the Registers of the Company of Stationers of London, 1554–1640 A.D. Ed. by E. ARBER, F.S.A. 4 Vols. 1875–1877.

RICHARD JONES was made free of the Stationers' Company, or, as it is entered in the *Register*, admitted " brother of this howse," 7th August 1564. *Transcript*, i. 278.

In the summer of 1566, occurs the following entry—

1. R. JONNES Recevyd of RYCHARD JONES for his lycense for prynting of a boke of *very pleasaunte Sonettes and storyes in myter*, by CLAMENT ROBYNSON. [*No sum as fee stated.*]

Trans. i. 313.

Not any portion of this First edition has, as yet, been verified. The fragment at *pp.* 15–16 may or may not belong to it.

The following ballads were *not* in this First Edition—

(a) Because the ballads themselves are registered at a later date.

In the years

22 July 1566–1567. *A fayne wolde I have a go[o]dly thynge to shewe vnto my ladye.* [see p. 50.] ... ... *Trans.* i. 340.

22 July 1567–1568. *A farewell to, Alas I lover you ouer well &c.* [See pp. 53 and 62.] ... ... *Trans.* i. 362. (This however may not have been the first appearance of this burden.)

22 July 1568–1569. *The Story of ij faythful Lovers &c.* [See pp. 30 and 46.] *Trans.* i. 386.

7 Nov. 1576. G. MANNINGTON's *Wœfull ballade.* [See p. 57.] *Trans.* ii. 324.

3 Sept. 1580.
18 Sept. 1580.
14 Dec. 1580. GREENSLEVES *and poems occasioned by it.* [See p. 17.]
13 Feb. 1581. *Trans.* ii. 376, 378, 384, 388, 400.
24 Aug. 1581.

10 March 1582.   *Callin o Custure me.*   [See p. 33.] ...   .   *Trans.* ii. 407.

(b) Because the ballad from which the following tune is named was registered also at a later date.

22 July 1567—22 July 1568.   *The godes of Love &c.* [See p. 36.]   *Trans.* i. 355.

Possibly a more detailed search would still further demonstrate the gradual growth of the Text up to the condition here reprinted.

2. 1584. London. 8vo.   See title at p. 1.

This unique imperfect copy was for many years in the possession of the Rev. T. CORSER of Stand Rectory, near Manchester: who refused to let the present Editor see it, not being in favour of making English Literature "as cheap as sixpenny chap-books." On the sale of this gentleman's magnificent Collection, it passed for some £9 or £10 into the British Museum Library.

3. A fragment of another Elizabethan edition discovered and identified by the Rev. J. W. EBSWORTH, M.A., while editing *The Bagford Ballads* in the British Museum for *The Ballad Society*, and reprinted by him in those *Ballads*, Part I, *Ed.* 1876. Mr. EBSWORTH thinks that the fragment is earlier than the present 1584 text.

Though unfortunately this leaf does not replace the missing one of No. 2: it is still useful in settling some of the readings on *p.* 49., which had been matters of dispute in consequence of the tender condition of the paper of the corresponding page in that volume.

4. 1815. London. 4to. *Heliconia*, comprising A selection of English poetry of the Elizabethan Age : &c.   3 Vols. Ed. by T. PARK. The *Handful, &c.*, is in Vol. ii.

5. 1871. Manchester. 4to. *Spenser Society's Issues, No. 8.* The *Handful, &c.* Sumptuously printed in facsimile, page for page, line for line, type for type, with *facsimile* ornaments &c. ; under the editorship of J[AMES] C[ROSSLEY, Esq, F.S.A.]

6. 15 Aug. 1878. Southgate, London, N.   8vo.   The present impression.

⁂ YARRATH JAMES had licenced to him on 13 Jan. 1581, *The parlour of Pleasaunte Delightes.*   *Trans.* ii. 387.

INTRODUCTION.

HE *Handefull of pleasant delites &c.* was one of the popular Song Books of the first half of Queen ELIZABETH's reign. The present text is that of a late impression of this Collection; which probably had already been reprinted more than once during the eighteen years which had now elapsed since its first appearance.

It is a Song Book rather than a Book of Poetry: so that had it originally appeared in 1596 instead of 1566 A.D., it would probably have been issued with the music: but at the time of its actual first publication, the London printers had not yet progressed sufficiently in their art to issue secular Songs with musical score.

RICHARD JONES, one of the minor publishers of his day, specially addicted himself to the production of ballads. This little book was originally made up of some of the more favourite songs that he had published &c.; with the natural variations or additions in subsequent impressions.

The principle of selection in the present text seems chiefly to have consisted in the exclusion of all poems on religious subjects, political affairs or distinguished persons; and also of all others on the monstrosities or wonderments of the hour to the description of which so many of the early Elizabethan ballads were devoted. In effect, to produce an attractive *Handful* of short songs "to solace the minds of those who delighted in music."

Being thus intended for singing, there is not a true Sonnet in the Collection.

An important feature of these early printed ballads is that they gave the names—either from their title, their first line, their burden or some prominent words therein—to the tunes to which they were first sung; by which names, these tunes are frequently quoted in the writings of SHAKESPEARE and his contemporaries.

In the Literary History of England, this Collection is the Fifth of the Eight Poetical Miscellanies which appeared in London between 1557 and 1602 A.D; the whole of which it is our desire, sooner or later, to reprint. The First of them, *TOTTEL's Miscellany* of 1557, we have already accomplished in the *English Reprints.*

The external history of this Text is also interesting in that we are indebted for it to an unique imperfect copy; and from the jealousy with which that was for so many years guarded from the public eye: so that—excepting, recently, the favoured readers of the issues of the *Spenser Society* of Manchester—the present is its first reappearance with any degree of accuracy in modern times.

Two notable illustrative quotations are here given: but there is every likelihood that now the text is made generally available, other points of contact with the Literature of the time will reward the inquiries of Students.

II.

HERE are two instances in which the influence of this Collection can be traced on the subsequent literature of our country.

1. SHAKESPEARE is supposed to have had the first poem, *the Nosegaie &c.* in mind, where in *HAMLET* he makes the distracted OPHELIA say—

Oph. There's rosemary, that's for remembrance; "pray you, love! remember!" and there is pansies, that's for thoughts.

Laer. A document in madness : thoughts and remembrance fitted.

Oph. There's fennel for you, and columbines; there's rue for you; and here's some for me; we may call it herb of grace o' Sundays; oh, you must wear your rue with a difference. There's a daisy; I would give you some violets, but they withered all when my father died; they say he made a good end.—*HAMLET, Act.* IV, *Sc.* 5. *Variorum Ed. of SHAKESPEARE*, by H. H. FURNESS, Vol. i. 345. *Ed.* 1877.

2. The second is a more marked acknowledgement. In *Eastward Hoe*, the joint production of GEORGE CHAPMAN, BEN JONSON and JOHN MARSTON, and printed in 1603; is the following parody of G. MANNINGTON's *sorrowfull Sonet*, as it is called at p. 57.

Quick. Sir, it is all the testimonie I shall leaue behinde me to the World, and my Maister, that I haue so offended.

Friend. Good Sir.

Qui. I writ it, when my spirits were opprest.

Pet. I, ile be sworne for you *Francis*.

Quic. It is in imitation of *Maningtons*; he that was hangd at *Cambridge*, that cut off the Horses head at a blowe.

Friend. So sir.

Quic. To the tune of *I waile in woe, I plunge in paine.*

Pet. An excellent Ditty it is, and worthy of a new tune.

Qui. *In* Cheapside *famous for Gold and Plate,*
Quicksiluer *I did dwel of late :*
I had a Master good, and kind,
That vvould haue vvrought me to his mind.
He bad me still, VVorke vpon that,

But alas I vvrought I knevv not vvhat.
He vvas a Touchstone black, but true :
And told me still, vvhat vvould ensue
Yet, vvoe is me, I vvould not learne,
I savv, alas, but could not discerne.

Friend. Excellent, excellent, well.

Gould. O let him alone, Hee is taken already.

Quic. *I cast my Coat, and Cap avvay,*
I went in silkes, and sattens gay,
False Mettall of good manners, I
Did dayly coine vnlavvfully.

I scorned my Master, being drunke,
I kept my Gelding, and my Punke,
And vvith a knight, sir Flash, *by name,*
(VVho novv is sory for the same.)

Pet. I thanke you *Francis*.

I thought by Sea to runne away,

| *But* Thames, *and Tempest did me stay.*

Touch. This cannot be fained sure. Heauen pardon my seuerity. *The ragged Colt, may proue a good Horse.*

Gould. How he listens ! and is transported? He has forgot mee.

Quic. Still Eastward hoe was all my word : | At last the blacke Oxe trode o' my foote,
But VVestward I had no regard. | And I saw then what longd vnto't.
Nor neuer thought, what would come after | Now cry I, Touchstone, touch me stil,
As did alas his youngest Daughter, | And make me currant by thy skill.

Touch. And I will doe it, *Francis*.

Wolfe. Stay him M. Deputy, now is the time, we shall loose the song else.

Frien. I protest it is the best that euer I heard.

Quick. How like you it Gentlemen ;

All. O admirable, sir !

Quic. This Stanze now following, alludes to the story of *Mannington* from whence I tooke my proiect for my inuention.

Fri[e]n[d]. Pray you goe on sir.

Quic. O Manington thy stories show, | That I may cut off the Horse-head of Sin.
Thou cutst a Horse-head off at a blow | And leaue his body in the dust
But I confesse, I haue not the force | Of sinnes high way and bogges of Lust,
For to cut off the head of a horse, | VVherby I may take Vertues purse,
Yet I desire this grace to winne, | And liue with her for better, for worse.

Fri[e]n[d]. Admirable sir, and excellently conceited.

Quick. Alas, sir.

Touch. Sonne *Golding* and M. *Wolfe*, I thank you: the deceipt is welcome, especially from thee whose charitable soule in this hath shewne a high point of wisdom and honesty. Listen. I am rauished with his Kepentance, and could stand here a whole prentiship to heare him.

Frien[d]. Forth good sir.

Quick. This is the last, and the *Farewell*.

Farewel Cheapside, farewel sweet trade | Auoide them as you would French scabs
Of Goldsmithes all, that neuer shall fade | Seeke not to goe beyond your Tether,
Farewell deare fellow Prentises all | But cut your Thongs vnto your Lether
And be you warned by my fall: | So shall you thriue by little and little,
Shun Vsurers, Bauds, and dice, and drabs. | Scape Tiborne, Counters, and the Spitle.

Touch. An scape them shalt thou my penitent, and dear *Frances.*

H. 3.

to sundrie new tunes.

All slayest the heart, whom thou maist help,

¶ A craggie Rock thy cradle was,
And Tygres milke sure was thy food :
Whereby Dame Nature brought to passe,
That like thy Nurse should be thy moode,
 Wilde and vnkind, cruell and fell,
 To flay the heart that loues thee well.

¶ The Crocodile with fained teares,
The Fisher not so oft beguiles :
As thou haste fild my simple eares,
To heare sweet words, full fraught with wiles
 That I may say, as I doo prooue,
 Wo worth the time I gan to loue.

¶ Sith thou haste vow'd to worke my wracke,
And haste no will my wealth to way,
Farewell vnkind, I will keep backe
Such toyes as may my health decay :
 And still will crie, as I haue cause,
 Fie vpon loue and all his lawes.

*The Louer being wounded with his Ladies
beautie, requireth mercy. To
the tune of Apelles.*

THe liuely sparkes of those two eyes,
My wounded heart hath set on fire :
And since I can no way deuise,
To stay the rage of my desire :
 with sighes and trembling teares I craue
 My deare, on me some pitty haue,
¶ In viewing thee, I tooke such ioy,
As one that sought his quiet rest :

D 2

Sonets and Histories,

Vntill I felt the feathered boy,
Ay flickering in my captiue breast :
  Since that time loe, in deep dispaire,
  All voyd of ioy, my time I weare.

¶ The wofull prisoner *Palemon,*
And *Troylus,* eke King *Pryamus,*
Constrain'd by loue did neuer mone,
As I (my deare) for the haue done,
  Let pitie then requite my paines
  My life and death in thee remaines.

¶ If constant loue may reape his hire,
And faith vnfained may purchase,
Great hope I haue to my desire,
Your gentle heart will grant me grace,
Till then (my deare) in few words plaine,
  In pensiue thoughts I shall remaine.

*The lamentation of a woman being wrongful-
lie defamed. To the tune of Damon and
Pythias.*

YOu Ladies falselie deem'd
  of any fault or crime,
Constraine your pensiue heartes to help
  this dolefull tune of mine :
  For spitefull men there are,
    That faults would faine espie :
  Alas, what heart would beare their talke,
    but willinglie would die :
¶ I waile oft times in woe,
    And curse mine houre of birth :
  Such slaunderous pangs doe me oppresse,
    when others ioy in mirth.

A Handefull
of pleasant delites,

Containing sundrie new Sonets
and delectable Histories, in
diuers kindes of Meeter.

Newly deuised to the newest tunes
that are now in vse, to be sung:
euerie Sonet orderly pointed
to his proper Tune

With new additions of certain Songs,
to verie late deuised Notes, not
commonly knowen, nor
vsed heretofore,

By Clement Robinson.
and diuers others.

¶ AT LONDON
Printed by Richard Ihones : dwelling at the signe of the Rose
and Crowne, neare
Holburne Bridge
1584.

The Printer to
the Reader.

YOu that in Musicke do delight
  your minds for to solace :
This little booke of Sonets m[ight]
  wel like you in that case,
Peruse it wel ere you passe by,
  here may you wish and haue,
Such pleasant songs to ech new tune,
  as lightly you can craue.
Or if fine Histories you would reade,
  you need not far to seek :
Within this booke such may you haue,
  as Ladies may wel like.
Here may you haue such pretie thinges,
  as women much desire :
Here may you haue of sundrie sorts,
  such Songs as you require.
Wherefore my friend, if you regard,
  such Songs to reade or heare :
Doubt not to buy this pretie Booke,
  the price is not so deare.

Farewell.

A Nosegaie alvvaies

sweet, for Louers to send for Tokens, of
loue, at Newyeres tide, or for fairings,
as they in their minds shall be disposed to write.

Nosegaie lacking flowers fresh,
 to you now I do send.
Desiring you to look thereon,
 when that you may intend :
For flowers fresh begin to fade,
 and *Boreas* in the field,
Euen with his hard coniealed frost,
 no better flowers doth yeeld :

¶ But if that winter could haue sprung,
 a sweeter flower than this,
I would haue sent it presently
 to you withouten misse :
Accept this then as time doth serue
 be thankful for the same,
Despise it not, but keep it well,
 and marke ech flower his name.

¶ *Lauander* is for louers true,
 which euermore be faine :
Desiring alwaies for to haue,
 some pleasure for their pain :

And when that they obtained haue,
    the loue that they require,
Then haue they al their perfect ioie,
    and quenched is the fire.

¶ *Rosemarie* is for remembrance,
    betweene vs daie and night :
Wishing that I might alwaies haue,
    you present in my sight.
And when I cannot haue,
    as I haue said before,
Then *Cupid* with his deadly dait,
    doth wound my heart full sore.

¶ *Sage* is for sustenance,
    that should mans life sustaine,
For I do stil lie languishing,
    continually in paine,
And shall do stil vntil I die,
    except thou fauour show :
My paine and all my greeuous smart,
    ful wel you do it know.

¶ *Fenel* is for flaterers,
    an euil thing it is sure :
But I haue alwaies meant truely,
    with constant heart most pure :
And will continue in the same,
    as long as life doth last,
Still hoping for a ioiful daie,
    when all our paines be past.

¶ *Violet* is for faithfulnesse,
    which in me shall abide :
Hoping likewise that from your heart,
    you wil not let it slide.
And wil continue in the same,
    as you haue nowe begunne :
And then for euer to abide,
    then you my heart haue wonne.

¶ *Time* is to trie me,
  as ech be tried must,
[?]tting you know while life doth last,
  I wil not be vniust,
And if I should I would to God,
  to hell my soule should beare.
And eke also that *Belzebub,*
  with teeth he should me teare.

¶ *Roses* is to rule me.
  with reason as you will,
For to be still obedient,
  your minde for to fulfill :
And thereto will not disagree,
  in nothing that you say :
But will content your mind truely,
  in all things that I may.

¶ *Ieliflowers* is for gentlenesse,
  which in me shall remaine :
Hoping that no sedition shal,
  depart our hearts in twaine.
As soone the sunne shal loose his course,
  the moone against her kinde,
Shall haue no light, if that I do
  once put you from my minde.

¶ *Carnations* is for gratiousnesse,
  marke that now by the way,
Haue no regard to flatterers,
  nor passe not what they say.
For they will come with lying tales,
  your eares for to fulfil :
In anie case do you consent,
  nothing vnto their wil.

¶ *Marigolds* is for marriage,
  that would our minds suffise,
Least that suspition of vs twaine,
  by anie meanes should rise :

As for my part, I do not care,
    my self I wil stil vse.
That all the women in the world,
    for you I will refuse.

¶ *Peniriall* is to print your loue,
    so deep within my heart :
That when you look this Nosegay on,
    my pain you may impart,
And when that you haue read the same,
    consider wel my wo,
Think ye then how to recompence,
    euen him that loues you so.

¶ *Cowsloppes* is for counsell,
    for secrets vs between,
That none but you and I alone,
    should know the thing we meane :
And if you wil thus wisely do,
    as I think to be best :
Then haue you surely won the field,
    and set my heart at rest.

[¶] I pray you keep this Nosegay wel,
    and set by it some store :
And thus farewel, the Gods thee guide,
    both now and euermore.
Not as the common sort do vse,
    to set it in your brest :
That when the smel is gone away,
    on ground he takes his rest.

FINIS.

L. Gibsons Tantara, wherin Danea welcommeth home her Lord Diophon from the war.

To the tune of, Down right Squire.

Ou Lordings, cast off your weedes of wo
   me thinks I heare
A trumpet shril which plain doth show
   my Lord is neare :
Tantara tara tantara,
   this trumpet glads our hearts,
Therefore to welcome home your King,
   you Lordings plaie your parts,
     Tantara tara tantara, &c.

¶ Harke harke, me thinkes I heare again,
   this trumpets voice,
He is at hand this is certaine,
   wherefore reioice.
Tantara tara tantara, &c.
   this trumpet still doth say,
With trumpets blast, all dangers past,
   doth shew in Marshall ray.
     [Tantara tara tantara, &c.]

¶ A ioifull sight my hearts delight,
   my *Diophon* deere :
Thy comely grace, I do embrace,
   with ioiful cheere :
Tantara tara tantara,
   what pleasant sound is this,
Which brought to me with victorie,
   my ioy and onely blisse.
     Tantara tara tantara, &c.

Diophon.

[¶] My Queene and wife, my ioy and life
    in whom I minde :
In euery part, the trustiest hart,
    that man can finde.
Tantara tara tantara,
    me thinks I heare your praise,
Your vertues race in euerie place,
    which trumpet so doth raise.
    Tantara tara tantara, &c.

[*Danea.*]

¶ Now welcome home to *Siria* soile,
    from battered field :
That valiantly thy foes did foile,
    with speare and shield :
Tantara tara tantara,
    me thinks I heare it still,
Thy sounding praise, abroad to raise,
    with trump that is most shrill,
    Tantara tara tantara, &c.

¶ If honour and fame, O noble Dame,
    such deeds do aske :
Then *Diophon* here to purchase fame,
    hath done this taske :
Tantara tara tantara,
    returnd he is againe,
To leade his life, with thee his wife,
    in ioie without disdaine.
    Tantara tara tantara, &c.

Finis

L. G.

¶ *A proper new Song made by a Student in Cambridge,   To the tune of I wish to see those happy daies.*

Which was once a happie wight,
    and hie in Fortunes grace :
And which did spend my golden prime,
    in running pleasures race,
        Am now enforst of late,
            contrariwise to mourne,
        Since fortune ioies, into annoies,
            my former state to turne.

¶ The toiling oxe, the horse, the asse,
    haue time to take their rest,
Yea all things else which Nature wrought,
    sometimes haue ioies in brest :
        Saue onelie I and such
            which vexed are with paine :
        For still in teares, my life it weares,
            and so I must remaine.

¶ How oft haue I in folded armes,
    enioied my delight,
How oft haue I excuses made,
    of her to haue a sight ?
        But now to fortunes wil,
            I caused am to bow.
        And for to reape a hugie heape,
            which youthful yeares did sow.

¶ Wherefore all ye which do as yet,
    remaine and bide behind :
Whose eies dame beauties blazing beams,
    as yet did neuer blind.
        Example let me be,
            to you and other more:
        Whose heauie hart, hath felt the smart,
            subdued by *Cupids* lore.

¶ Take heed of gazing ouer much,
   on Damsels faire vnknowne :
For oftentimes the Snake doth lie,
   with roses ouergrowde :
     And vnder fairest flowers,
       do noisome Adders lurke :
     Of whom take heed, I thee areed :
       least that thy cares they worke.

¶ What though that she doth smile on thee,
   perchance shee doth not loue :
And though she smack thee once or twice,
   she thinks thee so to prooue,
     And when that thou dost thinke,
       she loueth none but thee :
     She hath in store, perhaps some more,
       which so deceiued be,

¶ Trust not therefore the outward shew
   beware in anie case :
For good conditions do not lie,
   where is a pleasant face :
     But if it be thy chaunce,
       a louer true to haue :
     Be sure of this, thou shalt not misse,
       ech thing that thou wilt craue.

¶ And when as thou (good Reader) shalt
   peruse this scrole of mine :
Let this a warning be to thee,
   and saie a friend of thine,
     Did write thee this of loue,
       and of a zealous mind :
     Because that he sufficiently,
       hath tried the female kind.

¶ Here *Cambridge* now I bid farewell,
   adue to Students all :
Adue vnto the Colledges,
   and vnto *Gunuil* Hall :

And you my fellowes once,
    pray vnto *Ioue* that I
May haue releef, for this my grief,
    and speedie remedie.

¶ And that he shield you euerichone,
    from Beauties luring looks :
Whose baite hath brought me to my baine,
    and caught me from my Bꝏks :
        Wherefore, for you, my praier shall be,
            to send you better grace,
        That modestie with honestie,
            may guide your youthfull race.

Finis quod Thomas Richardson, sometime Student in Cambridge.

¶ *The scoffe of a Ladie, as pretie as may be,*
    to a yong man that went a wooing :
He went stil about her, and yet he went without her,
    because he was so long a dooing.

Ttend thee, go play thee,
Sweet loue I am busie :
    my silk and twist is not yet spun :
My Ladie will blame me,
If that she send for me,
    and find my worke to be vndun :
        How then ?
How shall I be set me ?
To say loue did let me ?
    Fie no, it will not fit me,
    It were no scuse for me.
    [It were no scuse for me.]

¶ If loue were attained,
My ioies were vnfained,
    my seame and silke wil take no hold :
Oft haue I beene warned,
By others proofe learned :
    hote wanton loue soone waxeth cold,
        Go now :

I say go pack thee,
Or my needle shal prick thee :
  Go seeke out Dame Idle :
  More fit for thy bridle,
  More fit for thy bridle.

¶ Wel worthie of blaming,
  For thy long detaining,
    all vaine it is that thou hast done :
Best now to be wandring,
Go vaunt of thy winning,
    and tell thy Dame what thou hast won :
      Say this :
Then say as I bade thee :
That the little dogge Fancie,
Lies chaste without moouing,
  And needeth no threatning,
  For feare of wel beating.
  For feare of wel beating.

¶ The boy is gone lurking,
  Good Ladies be working,
    dispatch a while that we had done,
The tide will not tarrie,
All times it doth varie,
    The day doth passe, I see the Sun,
      [? One line omitted by the Printer.]
The frost bites faire flowers,
Lets worke at due howres,
  Haste, haste, and be merie,
  Till our needles be werie.
  Till our needles be werie,

¶ Now Ladies be merie,
  Because you are werie :
    leaue worke I say, and get you home,
Your businesse is slacking,
Your louer is packing :
    your answer hath cut off his comb.
      How then ?

The fault was in him sir,
He wooed it so trim sir,
  Alas poor seelie fellow,
  Make much of thy pillow.
  Make much of thy pillow.

Finis.

An answer as pretie to the scof of his Lady,
by the yongman that came a wooing,
Wherein he doth flout her,
Being glad he went without her,
Misliking both her and her dooing.

ALas Loue, why chafe ye?
Why fret ye, why fume ye?
  to me it seemeth verie strange,
Me thinks ye misuse me,
So soone to refuse me,
  vnlesse you hope of better change:
    Wel, wel:
Wel now, I perceiue ye,
You are mindful to leaue me:
  Now sure it doth grieue me:
  That I am vnworthie:
  That I am vnworthie.

¶ I mean not to let ye, nor I can not forget ye,
  it wil not so out of my minde:
My loue is not daintie, I see you haue plenty
  that set so little by your friend.
Goe too spin on now I pray you, I list not to stay,
  I will goe play me:
  I am vnfit for you, &c.

[¶] Leaue off to flout now, and prick on your clout now
  you are a daintie Dame indeed,

And thogh of your taunting, I may make my vaunting
    as bad or worse than I shal speed :
Sweet heart, though now you forsake it.
I trust you will take it:
    and sure I spak[e] it, so fine as you make it, &c

[¶] Now wil I be trudging, without anie grudging
    I am content to giue you ground :
Good reson doth bind me, to leue you behind me,
    for you are better lost than found :
Go play, go seeke out Dame pleasure :
    You are a trim treasure,
    Wise women be daintie,
    Of fooles there be plentie, &c.

¶ If I might aduise ye, few words shuld suffice ye
    and yet you shold bestow them wel :
Maids must be manerly, not ful of scurility,
    wherein I see you do excel,
Farewel good *Nicibicetur,*
God send you a sweeter,
A lustie lim lifter, you are a trim shifter, &c.

Finis.

Peter Picks.

¶ Dame Beauties replie to the Louer late at
libertie : and now complaineth himselfe
to be her captiue, Intituled : Where is
the life that late I led.

THe life that erst thou ledst my friend,
    was pleasant to thine eies :
But now the losse of libertie,
    thou seemest to despise.
Where then thou ioiedst thy will,
    now thou doest grudge in heart :
Then thou no paine nor grief didst feele,
    but now thou pinest in smart.

What mooued thee vnto loue,
   expresse and tell the same :
Saue fancie thine, that heapt thy paine,
   thy follie learne to blame.

¶ For when thou freedome didst enioie,
   thou gauest thy selfe to ease,
And letst self-will the ruling beare,
   thy fancie fond to please :
Then stealing *Cupid* came,
   with bow and golden dart :
He struck the stroke, at pleasure he
   that now doth paine thy hart :
Blame not the Gods of loue,
   But blame thy self thou maist :
For freedome was disdaind of thee,
   and bondage more thou waiest.

¶ Who list, thou saist. to liue at rest,
   and freedome to possesse :
The sight of gorgeous Dames must shun,
   least loue do them distresse :
Thou blamest *Cupidoes* craft,
   who strikes in stealing sort :
And sets thee midst the princely Dames,
   of Beauties famous fort :
And meaning wel thou saiest,
   as one not bent to loue,
Then *Cupid* he constrains thee yeeld,
   as thou thy self canst prooue.

¶ Faire Ladies lookes in libertie,
   enlarged not thy paine :
Ne yet the sight of gorgeous Dames,
   could cause thee thus complaine.
It was thy self indeed,
   that causd thy pining woe,
Thy wanton wil, and idle minde,
   causd *Cupid* strike the blow :
Blame not his craft, nor vs

that Beauties darlings be,
Accuse thy selfe to seeke thy care,
thy fancie did agree.

¶ There is none thou saist, that can
more truely iudge the case :
Than thou that hast the wound receiu'de,
by sight of Ladies face.
Her beautie thee bewitcht,
thy minde that erst was free :
Her corps so comely framd, thou saiest,
did force thee to agree :
Thou gauest thy self it seemes,
her bondman to abide,
Before that her good willingnesse,
of thee were knowen and tride.

[¶] What iudgement canst thou giue :
how dost thou plead thy case :
It was not she that did thee wound,
although thou seest her face :
Ne could her beautie so,
inchaunt or vex thy sprites,
Ne feature hers so comely framde,
could weaken to thy wits.
But that thou mightest haue showne
the cause to her indeede,
Who spares to speak, thy self dost know,
doth faile of grace to speede.

¶ By this thou saiest, thou soughtst ye means
of torments that you beare,
By this thou wouldest men take heede,
and learne of loue to feare :
For taking holde thou telst,
to flie it is too late,
And no where canst thou shrowd thy self,
but Care must be thy mate.
Though loue do pleasure seeme,
yet plagues none such there are :
Therefore all louers now thou willst,
of liking to beware,

¶ Thy self hath sought the meane and way,
    and none but thou alone :
Of all the grief and care you beare,
    as plainely it is showne :
Then why should men take heed,
    thy counsell is vnfit :
Thou sparedst to speak, and faildst to speed,
    thy will had banisht wit.
And now thou blamest loue,
    and Ladies faire and free :
And better lost than found my frind,
    your cowards heart we see.

Finis.

I. P.

A new Courtly Sonet, of the Lady Green
sleeues. To the new tune of Greensleeues.

Greensleeues was all my ioy,
*   Greensleeues was my delight :*
Greensleeues was my hart of gold,
*   And who but Ladie Greensleeues.*

Las my loue, ye do me wrong,
    to cast me off discurteously :
And I haue loued you so long,
    Delighting in your companie.
    Greensleeues was all my ioy,
        Greensleeues was my delight :
    Greensleeues was my heart of gold,
        And who but Ladie Greensleeues.

¶ I haue been readie at your hand,
    to grant what euer you would craue.
I haue both waged life and land,
    your loue and good will for to haue.
    Greensleeues was all my ioy, &c.

¶ I bought thee kerchers to thy head,
    that were wrought fine and gallantly :
I kept thee both at boord and bed,
    Which cost my purse wel fauouredly,
        Greensleeues was al my ioie, &c.

¶ I bought thee peticotes of the best,
    the cloth so fine as fine might be :
I gaue thee iewels for thy chest,
    and all this cost I spent on thee.
        Greensleeues was all my ioie, &c.

¶ Thy smock of silk, both faire and white,
    with gold embrodered gorgeously :
Thy peticote of Sendall right :
    and thus I bought thee gladly.
        Greensleeues was all my ioie, &c.

¶ Thy girdle of gold so red,
    with pearles bedecked sumptuously :
The like no other lasses had,
    and yet thou wouldst not loue me,
        Greensleeues was all my ioy, &c.

¶ Thy purse and eke thy gay guilt kniues,
    thy pincase gallant to the eie :
No better wore the Burgesse wiues,
    and yet thou wouldst not loue me.
        Greensleeues was all my ioy, &c.

¶ Thy crimson stockings all of silk,
    with golde all wrought aboue the knee,
Thy pumps as white as was the milk,
    and yet thou wouldst not loue me.
        Greensleeues was all my ioy, &c.

¶ Thy gown was of the grossie green,
    thy sleeues of Satten hanging by :
Which made thee be our haruest Queen,
    and yet thou wouldst not loue me.
        Greensleeues was all my ioy, &c.

¶ Thy garters fringed with the golde,
   And siluer aglets hanging by,
Which made thee blithe for to beholde,
   And yet thou wouldst not loue me.
      Greensleeues was all my ioy, &c.

¶ My gayest gelding I thee gaue,
   To ride where euer liked thee,
No Ladie euer was so braue,
   And yet thou wouldst not loue me.
      Greensleeues was all my ioy, &c.

¶ My men were clothed all in green,
   And they did euer wait on thee :
Al this was gallant to be seen,
   and yet thou wouldst not loue me.
      Greensleeues was all my ioy, &c.

¶ They set thee vp, they took thee downe,
   they serued thee with humilitie,
Thy foote might not once touch the ground,
   and yet thou wouldst not loue me.
      Greensleeues was all my ioy, &c.

¶ For euerie morning when thou rose,
   I sent thee dainties orderly :
To cheare thy stomack from all woes,
   and yet thou wouldst not loue me.
      Greensleeues was all my ioy, &c.

¶ Thou couldst desire no earthly thing.
   But stil thou hadst it readily :
Thy musicke still to play and sing,
   And yet thou wouldst not loue me.
      Greensleeues was all my ioy, &c.

¶ And who did pay for all this geare,
   that thou didst spend when pleased thee ?
Euen I that am reiected here,
   and thou disdainst to loue me.
      Greensleeues was all my ioy, &c.

¶ Wel, I wil pray to God on hie,
    that thou my constancie maist see :
And that yet once before I die,
    thou wilt vouchsafe to loue me.
        Greensleeues was all my ioy, &c.

¶ Greensleeues now farewel adue
    God I pray to prosper thee :
For I am stil thy louer true,
    come once againe and loue me.
        Greensleeues was all my ioy, &c.

          Finis.

*A proper sonet, wherin the Louer dolefully sheweth
his grief to his L[ady]. and requireth pity.*

To the tune of, Row wel ye Marriners.

AS one without refuge,
    For life doth pleade with panting breath
And rufully the Iudge,
    Beholds (whose doome grants life or death,)
So fare I now my onelie Loue,
Whom I tender as Turtle Doue,
    Whose tender looks (O ioly ioy)
    Shall win me sure your louing boy :
    Faire lookes, sweet Dame,
    Or else (alas) I take my bane :
Nice talke, coying,
Wil bring me sure to my ending,

¶ Too little is my skil,
    By pen (I saie) my loue to paint,   .
And when that my good will,
    My tong wold shew, my heart doth faint :
Sith both the meanes do faile therefore,
My loue for to expresse with lore :
    The torments of my inward smart.
    You may well gesse within your hart :

Wherefore, sweet wench,
Some louing words, this heat to quench
Fine smiles, smirke lookes,
And then I neede no other lookes,

¶ Your gleams hath gript the hart,
  alas within my captiue breast:
O how I feele the smart,
  And how I find my griefe increast:
My fancie is so fixt on you,
That none away the same can do:
    My deer vnlesse you it remooue:
    Without redresse I die for loue,
    Lament with me,
    Ye Muses nine, where euer be,
My life I loth,
My Ioies are gone, I tel you troth.

¶ All Musicks solemne sound,
  Of song, or else of instrument:
Me thinks they do resound,
  With doleful tunes, me to lament,
And in my sleep vnsound, alas,
Me thinks such dreadful things to passe:
    that out I crie in midst of dreames,
    Wherwith my tears run down as streams,
    O Lord, think I,
    She is not here that should be by:
What chance is this,
That I embrace that froward is?

¶ The Lions noble minde,
  His raging mood (you know) oft staies,
When beasts do yeeld by kinde,
  On them (forsooth) he neuer praies:
Then sithence that I am your thrall,
To ease my smart on you I call.
    A bloudie conquest is your part,
    To kill so kind a louing heart:

Alas remorce,
Or presently I die perforce :
God grant pitie,
Within your breast now planted be.

¶ As nature hath you deckt,
   with worthie gifts aboue the rest,
So to your praise most great,
   Let pitie dwell within your brest,
That I may saie with heart and wil,
Lo, this is she that might me kil :
   For why ? in hand she held the knife,
   And yet (forsooth) she saued my life.
   Hey-ho, darling :
   With lustie loue, now let vs sing,
Plaie on, Minstrel,
My Ladie is mine onelie girle.

The Historie of Diana and Actæon.

To the Quarter Braules.

Iana and her darlings deare,
Walkt once as you shall heare :
Through woods and waters cleare,
   themselues to play :
The leaues were gay and green,
And pleasant to be seen :
They went the trees between,
   in coole aray,
So long, that at the last they found a place,
   of waters full cleare :
So pure and faire a Bath neuer was
   found many a yeare.
There shee went faire and gent,
Her to sport, as was her wonted sort :
   In such desirous sort :
   Thus goeth the report :
Diana dainteously began her selfe therein to bathe
   And her body for to laue,
   So curious and braue.

¶ As they in water stood,
  Bathing their liuelie blood:
  Acteon in the wood,
    chaunst to come by:
  And vewed their bodies bare,
  Maruailing what they weare,
  And stil deuoid of care,
    on them cast his eie:
  But when the Nymphs had perceiued him,
    aloud then they cried,
  Enclosed her, and thought to hide her skin,
    which he had spied:
  But too true I tell you,
    She seene was,
    For in height she did passe,
    Ech Dame of her race.
    Harke then *Acteons* case:
  When *Diana* did perceue, where *Acteon* did stand,
    She took bowe in her hand,
    And to shoot she began.

¶ As she began to shoot, *Acteon* ran about,
  To hide he thought no boote,
    his sights were dim:
  And as he thought to scape,
  Changed was *Acteons* shape, .
  Such was vnluckie fate,
    yeelded to him:
  For *Diana* brought it thus to passe,
    and plaied her part,
  So that poore *Acteon* changed was
    to a hugie Hart,
  And did beare, naught but haire:
    In this change,
    Which is as true as strange,
    And thus did he range,

                                    Abroad

[*Leaf* B. vj *is wanting.*]

[*Leaf* B. vj *is wanting.*]

So that his sorrowes importunate,
Had ended his life incontinent,
Had not Lady *Venus* grace, Lady Lady,
Pitied her poore seruants case,
          My deer Ladie.

¶ For when she saw the torments strong,
Wherewith the Knight was sore opprest,
Which he God knowes had suffered long,
Al through this Ladies mercilesse,
Of their desires she made exchange,
          Ladie, Ladie.
And wrought a myracle most strange,
          My deer Ladie.

¶ So that this Ladie faithfully,
Did loue this Knight aboue all other :
And he vnto the contrarie,
Did hate her then aboue all measure,
And pitifull she did complaine : ladie, ladie.
Requiring fauour, and might not obtaine.
          My deer ladie.

¶ But when she saw, that in no case,
She might vnto his loue attaine :
And that she could not finde some grace,
To ease her long enduring paine,
And yat his hart wold not remoue, Lady, ladie
Without all cure [s]he died for loue,
          My deer.[ladie.]

¶ Besides these matters maruelous,
One other thing I wil you tell :
Of one whose name was *Narcissus*,
A man whose beautie doth excel.
Of natures gifts he had no misse, Lady, lady
He had ye whole of beauties blisse,
          My deere.[ladie.]

¶ So that out of manie a far Countrey,
I reade of manie a woman faire,
Did come this *Narcissus* to see,
Who perished when they came there,

Through his default I say in fine, lady, lady
Who vnto loue would not incline.
            My deer.[ladie.]

¶ Whose disobedience vnto loue,
  When vnto *Venus* it did appeare.
  How that his hart would not remoue,
  She punisht him as you shal heare :
  A thing most strange forsooth it was,
            Ladie, Ladie.
  Now harken how it came to passe,
            My deer.[ladie.]

¶ For when he went vpon a daie,
  With other mo in strange disguise,
  Himself forsooth he did aray
  In womans attire of a new deuise,
  And ouer a bridge as he did go, Ladie, ladie.
  In the water he sawe his own shadow,
            My.[deer ladie.]

¶ Which when he did perceiue and see,
  A Ladie faire he saith it seemeth :
  Forgat himself that it was he,
  And iudgde that it was *Dianaes* Nymph,
  Who in the waters in such fashion, Lady, la[dy]
  Did vse themselues for recreation,
            My deer.[ladie.]

¶ And through the beautie of whose looks,
  Taken he was with such fond desire,
  That after manie humble sutes,
  Incontinent he did aspire.
  Vnto her grace him to refer, Ladie, Ladie
  Trusting yat mercie was in her,
            My deer, &c.

¶ With armes displaid he took his race,
  And leapt into the riuer there,
  And thought his Ladie to imbrace,

Being of himselfe, deuoid of feare,
And there was drownd without redresse, Ladie, Ladie.
His crueltie rewarded was,
    with such follie.

¶ Loe, hereby you may perceiue,
How *Venus* can, and if she please,
Her disobedient Subiects grieue,
And make them drinke their owne disease,
Wherfore rebel not I you wish, Lady, lady.
Least that your chaunce be worse than this,
    if worse may be.

Finis.

The Louer complaineth the losse of his Ladie
To Cecilia Pauin.

Eart, what makes thee thus to be,
    in extreame heauinesse ?
If care do cause all thy distresse,
Why seekest thou not some redresse,
    to ease thy carefulnesse ?
Hath *Cupid* stroke in Venerie,
Thy wofull corps in ieoperdie :
    right wel then may I sob and crie,
Til that my Mistresse deer, my faith may trie
Why would I cloake from her presence,
    My loue and faithfull diligence ?
    And cowardly thus to die.
    And cowardly thus to die.

¶ 'No no, I wil shew my woe,
    in this calamitie.
To her whom Nature shapte so free :
With all *Dianaes* chastitie,
    or *Venus* rare beautie :
Then shall I brace felicitie,
And liue in all prosperitie.

then leaue off this woe, let teares go,
thou shalt embrace thy Ladie deer with ioy.
In these thy armes so louingly,
As *Paris* did faire *Helenie*.
 By force of blinded boy.
 By force of blinded boy.

¶ If *Venus* would grant vnto me,
 such happinesse :
As she did vnto *Troylus*,
By help of his friend *Pandarus*,
 To *Cressids* loue who worse,
 Than all the women certainly :
 That euer liued naturally.
Whose slight falsed faith, the storie saith,
Did breed by plagues, her great and sore distresse,
 For she became so leprosie,
 That she did die in penurie :
 Because she did transgresse.
 Because she did transgresse.

¶ If she, I saie, wil me regard,
 in this my ieoperdie,
.I wil shew her fidelitie,
And eke declare her curtesie,
 to Louers far and nie :
O heart how happie shouldst thou be,
When my Ladie doth smile on me :
 Whose milde merie cheare,
 Wel driue away feare,
Cleane from my brest, and set ioy in ye place
 when I shall kisse so tenderly :
Her fingers small and slenderly,
 which doth my heart solace, &c.

[¶] Therefore ye amorous imps who burne
 so stil in *Cupids* fire,
Let this the force of my retire
Example be to your desire,
 That so to loue aspire :
 For I did make deniance,
 And set her at defiance :

Which made me full wo, it chanced so,
Because I look at my mistresse so coy :
Therefore, when she is merily
Disposed, look you curteously :
    Receiue her for your ioy.
    Receiue her for your ioy.

Finis.

I. Tomson.

The Louer compareth some subtile Suters
to the Hunter. *To the tune of the Painter.*

Hen as the Hunter goeth out,
    with hounds in brace.
The Hart to hunt, and set about,
    with wilie trace,
He doth it more to see and view,
Her wilinesse (I tell you true.)
Her trips and skips, now here, now there,
With squats and flats, which hath no pere.

¶ More than to win or get the game
        to beare away :
He is not greedie of the same,
        (thus Hunters saie :
So some men hunt by hote desire,
To *Venus* Dames, and do require
With fauor to haue her, or els they wil die,
they loue her, and prooue her, and wot ye why ?

¶ Forsooth to see her subtilnesse, and wily way.
    When they (God knows) mean nothing lesse
        than they do say :
    For when they see they may her win,
    They leaue then where they did begin.
        they prate and make the matter nice,
        And leaue her in fooles paradice.

¶ Wherefore of such (good Ladie now)
    wisely beware,
Least flinging fancies in their brow,
    do breed you care :
And at the first giue them the checke,
Least they at last giue you the geck,
    And scornfully disdaine ye then,
    In faith there are such kind of men.

¶ But I am none of those indeed,
    beleeue me now :
I am your man if you me need,
    I make a vow :
To serue you without doublenesse :
With feruent heart my owne mistresse,
    Demaund me, commaund me,
    what please ye, and whan,
I wil be stil readie, as I am true man.

A new Sonet of Pyramus and Thisbie.

To the, Downe right Squier.

Ou Dames (I say) that climbe the mount
    of *Helicon,*
Come on with me, and giue account,
    what hath been don :
Come tell the chaunce ye Muses all,
    and dolefull newes,
Which on these Louers did befall,
    which I accuse.
In *Babilon* not long agone,
    a noble Prince did dwell :
whose daughter bright dimd ech ones sight,
    so farre she did excel.

¶ An other Lord of high renowne,
    who had a sonne :
And dwelling there within the towne,
    great loue begunne :

Pyramus this noble Knight,
    I tel you true :
Who with the loue of *Thisbie* bright,
    did cares renue :
It came to passe, their secrets was,
    beknowne vnto them both :
And then in minde, they place do finde,
    where they their loue vnclothe.

¶ This loue they vse long tract of time,
    till it befell :
At last they promised to meet at prime,
    by *Minus* well :
Where they might louingly imbrace,
    in loues delight :
That he might see his *Thisbies* face,
    and she his sight :
In ioyful case, she approcht the place,
    where she her *Pyramus*
Had thought to viewd, but was renewd,
    to them most dolorous.

¶ Thus while she staies for *Pyramus*,
    there did proceed :
Out of the wood a Lion fierce,
    made *Thisbie* dreed :
And as in haste she fled awaie,
    her Mantle fine :
The Lion tare in stead of praie,
    till that the time
That *Pyramus* proceeded thus,
    and see how lion tare
The Mantle this of *Thisbie* his,
    he desperately doth fare.

¶ For why he thought the lion had,
    faire *Thisbie* slaine.
And then the beast with his bright blade,
    he slew certaine :
Then made he mone and said alas,

(O wretched wight)
Now art thou in a woful case
    for *Thisbie* bright :
Oh Gods aboue, my faithfull loue
    shal neuer faile this need :
For this my breath by fatall death,
    shal weaue *Atropos* threed.

¶ Then from his sheathe he drew his blade,
    and to his hart
He thrust the point, and life did vade,
    with painfull smart :
Then *Thisbie* she from cabin came
    with pleasure great,
And to the well apase she ran,
    there for to treat :
And to discusse, to *Pyramus*
    of al her former feares.
And when slaine she, found him truly,
    she shed foorth bitter teares.

¶ When sorrow great that she had made,
    she took in hand
The bloudie knife, to end her life,
    by fatall hand.
You Ladies all, peruse and see,
    the faithfulnesse,
How these two Louers did agree,
    to die in distresse :
You Muses waile, and do not faile,
    but still do you lament :
These louers twaine, who with such paine,
    did die so well content.

Finis.

I. Thomson.

A Sonet of a Louer in the praise of his lady.

To Calen o Custure me: sung at euerie lines end.

Hen as I view your comly grace, *Ca.* &c
Your golden haires, your angels face:
Your azured veines much like the skies,
Your siluer teeth, your Christall eies.
 Your Corall lips, your crimson cheeks,
 That Gods and men both loue and leekes.

¶ Your pretie mouth with diuers gifts,
Which driueth wise men to their shifts:
So braue, so fine, so trim, so yong,
With heauenlie wit and pleasant tongue,
 That *Pallas* though she did excell,
 Could frame ne tel a tale so well.

¶ Your voice so sweet, your necke so white,
your bodie fine and small in sight:
Your fingers long so nimble be,
To vtter foorth such harmonie,
 As all the Muses for a space:
 To sit and heare do giue you place.

¶ Your pretie foot with all the rest,
That may be seene or may be gest:
Doth beare such shape, that beautie may
Giue place to thee and go her way:
 And *Paris* nowe must change his doome,
 For *Venus* lo must giue thee roome.

¶ Whose gleams doth heat my hart as fier,
Although I burne, yet would I nier:
Within my selfe then can I say:
The night is gone, behold the day:
 Behold the star so cleare and bright,
 As dimmes the sight of *Phœbus* light:

¶ Whose fame by pen for to discriue,
Doth passe ech wight that is aliue:
Then how dare I with boldned face,
Presume to craue or wish your grace ?
    And thus amazed as I stand,
    Not feeling sense, nor moouing hand.

¶ My soule with silence moouing sense,
Doth wish of God with reuerence,
Long life, and vertue you possesse :
To match those gifts of worthinesse,
    And loue and pitie may be spide,
    To be your chief and onely guide.

¶ *A proper Sonet, Intituled, Maid, wil you*
marrie. To the Blacke Almaine.

Aid, wil you marie ?   I pray sir tarie,
    I am not disposed to wed a :
For he yat shal haue me, wil neuer deny me
    he shal haue my maidenhed a.
Why then you wil not wed me ?
No sure sir I haue sped me,
    You must go seeke some other wight,
    That better may your heart delight.
For I am sped I tell you true,
beleue me it greues me, I may not haue you,
To wed you and bed you as a woman shold be

¶ For if I could, be sure I would,
    consent to your desire :
I would not doubt, to bring about
    ech thing you would require :
But promise now is made,
Which cannot be staide :
    It is a womans honestie,
    To keep her promise faithfully.
And so I do meane til death to do,
Consider and gather, that this is true :
Choose it, and vse it, the honester you.

¶ · But if you seek, for to misleeke,
　　with this that I haue done :
Or else disdaine, that I so plaine
　　this talke with you haue begone :
Farewell I wil not let you,
He fisheth well that gets you,
　　And sure I thinke your other friend,
　　Wii prooue a Cuckold in the end :
But he wil take heed if he be wise,
To watch you and catch you, with *Argus* eies,
Besetting and letting your wonted guise.

¶ Although the Cat doth winke a while,
　　yet sure she is not blinde :
It is the waie for to beguile,
　　the Mice that run behind :
And if she see them running,
Then straightway she is comming :
　　Vpon their head she claps her foote,
　　To striue with her it is no boote.
The seelie poore Mice dare neuer play,
She catcheth and snatcheth them euery day,
Yet whip they, and skip they, when she is away.

¶ And if perhaps they fall in trap,
　　to death then must they yeeld :
They were better then, to haue kept their den
　　than straie abroad the field :
But they that will be ranging,
Shall soone repent their changing :
　　And so shall you ere it be long,
　　Wherefore remember well my song :
And do not snuffe though I be plaine,
But cherily, merily, take the same.
For huffing and snuffing deserueth blame.

¶ For where you say you must obay,
　　the promise you haue made,
So sure as I wil neuer flie,
　　from that I haue said :

Therefore to them I leaue you,
Which gladly wil receiue you :
   You must go choose some other mate,
   According to your own estate.
For I do meane to liue in rest,
Go seek you, and leek you an other guest,
And choose him, and vse him, as you like best.

The ioy of Virginitie : to, The Gods of loue

Iudge and finde, how God doth minde,
   to furnish, to furnish
      his heauenly throne aboue,
  With virgins pure, this am I sure,
  without misse, without misse :
   with other Saints he doth loue :
It is allowed as you may reade,
And eke auowed by *Paul* indeede,
  Virginitie is accepted,
   a thing high in Gods sight :
  Though marriage is selected,
   a thing to be most right :
yet must I praise *Virginitie*,
For I would faine a Virgin be.

¶ You Virgins pure, your selues assure,
  and credite, and credite :
   great ioy you shall possesse,
Which I (God knows) cannot disclose,
  nor spreade it, nor spreade it,
   ne yet by pen expresse.
Nor halfe the ioies that you shall finde,
I can not iudge for you assignde :
  When hence your ghost shall yeelded be,
   into the throne of blisse :
  In chaste and pure Virginitie,
   for thought or deed ywisse :
Wher you shal raign, with God on hie
For euermore eternally.

¶ And when doubtlesse, you shal possesse,
    with Iesus, with Iesus,
      these ioies celestiall.
Then Ladie Fame, wil blaze your name,
    amongst vs, amongst vs,
      which then on earth raigne shal.
She wil resound in euerie coast,
By trumpet sound, and wil you boast ?
    So that although you do depart
      This mortall life so vaine :
    Your chastitie in euerie heart,
      by memorie shall remaine.
But hard it is, I saie no more,
To finde an hundreth in a score.

Finis.

¶ *A warning for Wooers, that they be not
ouer hastie, nor deceiued with womens
beautie, To, Salisburie Plaine.*

YE louing wormes come learne of me
The plagues to leaue that linked be :
The grudge, the grief, the gret anoy,
The fickle faith, the fading ioy :
    in time, take heed,
In fruitlesse soile sow not thy seed :
    buie not, with cost,
    the thing that yeelds but labour lost.

¶ If *Cupids* dart do chance to light,
    So that affection dimmes thy sight,
    Then raise vp reason by and by,
    With skill thy heart to fortifie
      Where is a breach,
    Oft times too late doth come the Leach :
      Sparks are put out,
      when fornace flames do rage about.

¶ Thine owne delay must win the field,
  When lust doth leade thy heart to yeeld:
  When steed is stolne, who makes al fast,
  May go on foot for al his haste:
      In time shut gate,
  For had I wist, doth come too late,
      Fast bind, fast find,
      Repentance alwaies commeth behind.

¶ The *Syrens* times [*tunes*] oft time beguiles,
  So doth the teares of Crocodiles:
  But who so learnes *Vlysses* lore,
  May passe the seas, and win the shore.
      Stop eares, stand fast,
  Through *Cupids* trips, thou shalt him cast:
      Flie baits, shun hookes,
      Be thou not snarde with louely lookes.

¶ Where *Venus* hath the maisterie,
  There loue hath lost her libertie:
  where loue doth win the victorie,
 _ The fort is sackt with crueltie.
      First look, then leap,
  In suretie so your shinnes you keepe:
      The snake doth sting,
      That lurking lieth with hissing.

¶ Where *Cupids* fort hath made a waie,
  There graue aduise doth beare no swaie,
  Where Loue doth raigne and rule the roste,
  There reason is exilde the coast:
  Like all, loue none, except ye vse discretion,
  First try, then trust, be not deceiued with sinful lust,

¶ Marke *Priams* sonne, his fond deuise
  When *Venus* did obtaine the price:
  For *Pallas* skil and *Iunoes* strength,
  He chose that bred his bane at length.
  Choos[e] wit, leaue wil, let *Helen* be with *Paris* stil:
  Amis[s] goeth al, wher fancie forceth fooles to fall.

¶ Where was there found a happier wight,
Than *Troylus* was til loue did light?
What was the end of *Romeus*.
Did he not die like *Piramus*
who baths in blis? let him be mindful of *Iphis*
who seeks to plese, may ridden be like *Hercules*.

¶ I lothe to tel the peeuish brawles,
And fond delights of *Cupids* thrawles,
Like momish mates of *Midas* mood,
They gape to get that doth no good:
Now down, now vp, as tapsters vse to tosse ye Cup
One breedeth ioy, another breeds as great anoy

¶ Some loue for wealth, and some for hue,
And none of both these loues are true.
For when the Mil hath lost hir sailes,
Then must the Miller lose his vailes:
    Of grasse commeth hay,
And flowers faire wil soon decay:
    Of ripe commeth rotten,
    In age al beautie is forgotten.

[¶] Some loueth too hie, and some too lowe,
And of them both great griefs do grow,
And some do loue the common sort:
And common folke vse common sport.
    Looke not too hie,
Least that a chip fall in thine eie:
    But hie or lowe,
    Ye may be sure she is a shrow.

¶ But sirs, I vse to tell no tales,
Ech fish that swims doth not beare scales,
In euerie hedge I finde not thornes:
Nor euerie beast doth carrie hornes:
    I saie not so,
That euerie woman causeth wo:
    That were too broad,
    Who loueth not venom must shun the tode.

¶ Who vseth still the truth to tel,
  May blamed be though he saie wel :
Say Crowe is white, and snowe is blacke,
Lay not the fault on womans backe,
    Thousands were good,
But few scapte drowning in *Noes* flood :
    Most are wel bent,
    I must say so, least I be shent.

Finis.

¶ *An excellent Song of an outcast Louer.*

To, All in a Garden green.

Y fancie did I fixe,
  in faithful forme and frame :
in hope ther shuld no blustring blast
  haue power to moue the same.

  ¶ And as the Gods do know,
      and world can witnesse beare :
    I neuer serued other Saint,
      nor Idoll other where.

  ¶ But one, and that was she,
      whom I in heart did shrine :
    And make account that pretious pearle,
      and iewel rich was mine.

  ¶ No toile, nor labour great,
      could wearie me herein :
    For stil I had a *Iasons* heart,
      the golden fleece to win.

  ¶ And sure my sute was hearde,
      I spent no time in vaine :
    A grant of friendship at her hand,
      I got to quite my paine.

[¶] With solemne vowe and othe.
    was knit the True-loue knot,
And friendly did we treat of loue,
    as place and time we got.

¶ Now would we send our sighes,
    as far as they might go,
Now would we worke with open signes,
    to blaze our inward wo.

¶ Now rings and tokens too,
    renude our friendship stil,
And ech deuice that could be wrought,
    exprest our plaine goodwill,

[¶] True meaning went withall,
    it cannot be denide :
Performance of the promise past,
    was hopte for of ech side :

¶ And lookt for out of hand :
    such vowes did we two make,
As God himself had present been,
    record thereof to take.

¶ And for my part I sweare,
    by all the Gods aboue,
I neuer thought of other friend,
    nor sought for other loue.

¶ The same consent in her,
    I saw ful oft appeare,
If eies could see, or head could iudge,
    or eare had power to heare.

¶ Yet loe wordes are but winde,
    an other new come guest,
Hath won her fauour (as I feare)
    as fancies rise in brest.

[¶] Her friend that wel deserues,
  is out of countenaunce quite,
She makes the game to see me shoot,
  while others hit the white.

[¶] He may wel beat the bush,
  as manie thousands doo :
And misse the birds, and haply loose
  his part of feathers too.

¶ He hops without the ring,
  yet daunceth on the trace,
When some come after soft and faire,
  a heauie hobling pace.

¶ In these vnconstant daies,
  such troth these women haue :
As wauering as the aspen leaf
  they are, so God me saue.

¶ For no deserts of men
  are wei[ghe]d, what ere they be :
For in a mood their minds are led
  with new delights we see.

¶ The guiltlesse goeth to wrack,
  the gorgeous peacocks gay :
They do esteem vpon no cause,
  and turne their friends away.

¶ I blame not al for one,
  some flowers grow by the weeds,
Some are as sure as lock and key,
  and iust of words and deeds.

¶ And yet of one I waile,
  of one I crie and plaine :
And for her sake shall neuer none,
  so nip my heart againe :

¶ If for offence or fault,
　　I had been floong at heele :
The lesse had been my bitter smart,
　　and gnawing greefe I feele.

¶ But being once reteind,
　　a friend by her consent :
And after that to be disdaind,
　　when best good will I ment,

¶ I take it nothing well,
　　for if my power could show,
With Larum bel and open crie,
　　the world should throughly know.

The complaint of a woman Louer,
To the tune of, Raging loue.

Hough wisdom wold I shold refrain,
My heaped cares here to vnfold :
Good Ladies yet my inward paine,
So pricketh me I haue no holde :
　　But that I must my griefe bewray,
　　Bedewed in teares with doleful tunes,
　　That you may heare, and after say,
　　Loe, this is she whom loue consumes.

¶ My grief doth grow by my desire.
To fancie him that stormes my woe :
He naught regards my flaming fire,
Alas why doth he serue me so?
　　Whose fained teares I did beleeue,
　　And wept to heare his wailing voice,
　　But now, alas, too soon I preeue
　　Al men are false, there is no choice.

¶ Had euer woman such reward,
At anie time for her goodwill ?
Had euer woman hap so hard,
So cruelly for loue to spill ?

What paps (alas) did giue him food,
That thus vnkindly workes my wo ?
What beast is of so cruell moode,
to hate the hart that loues him so ?

¶ Like as the simple Turtle true,
In mourning groanes I spend the day :
My daily cares night dooth renew,
To thinke how he did me betray :
   And when my weary limmes wold rest,
   My sleepe vnsound hath dreadfull dreams,
   Thus greeuous greefes my hart doth wrest
   That stil mine eies run down like streams :

¶ And yet, full oft it dooth me good,
To haunt the place where he hath beene,
To kisse the ground whereon he stoode,
When he (alas) my loue did win.
   To kisse the Bed wheron we laye ?
   Now may I thinke vnto my paine,
   O blisfull place full oft I say :
   Render to me my loue againe,

¶ But all is lost that may not be,
Another dooth possesse my right :
His cruell hart, disdaineth me,
New loue hath put the olde, to flight :
   He loues to see my watered eyes,
   and laughes to see how I do pine :
   No words can well my woes comprise,
   alas what griefe is like to mine ?

¶ You comly Dam[e]s, beware by me,
To rue sweete words of fickle trust :
For I may well example be,
How filed talke oft prooues vniust
   But sith deceipt haps to my pay,
   Good Ladyes helpe my dolefull tunes,
   That you may here and after say :
   Loe this is she whom loue consumes.

*A proper sonet, Intituled: I smile to see how
you deuise.   To anie pleasant tune.*

 Smile to see how you deuise,
New masking nets my eies to bleare:
your self you cannot so disguise:
But as you are, you must appeare.

¶ your priuie winkes at boord I see,
   And how you set your rouing mind:
   your selfe you cannot hide from me,
   Although I wincke, I am not blind.

¶ The secret sighs and fained cheare,
   That oft doth paine thy carefull brest:
   To me right plainly doth appeare,
   I see in whom thy hart doth rest.

¶ And though thou makest a fained vow,
   That loue no more thy heart should nip,
   yet think I know as well as thou,
   The fickle helm doth guide the ship.

¶ The Salamander in the fire,
   By course of kinde doth bathe his limmes:
   The floting Fish taketh his desire,
   In running streams whereas he swimmes.

¶ So thou in change dost take delight,
   Ful wel I know thy slipperie kinde:
   In vaine thou seemst to dim my sight,
   Thy rowling eies bewraieth thy minde.

¶ I see him smile that doth possesse
   Thy loue which once I honoured most:
   If he be wise, he may well gesse,
   Thy loue soon won, wil soon be lost.

¶ And sith thou canst no man intice,
That he should stil loue thee alone :
Thy beautie now hath lost her price,
I see thy sauorie s[c]ent is gone.

¶ Therefore leaue off thy wonted plaie,
But, as thou art, thou wilt appeare,
Vnlesse thou canst deuise a waie,
To dark the Sun that shines so cleare.

¶ And keep thy friend that thou hast won,
In trueth to him thy loue supplie,
Least he at length as I haue done,
Take off thy Belles and let thee flie.

A Sonet of two faithfull Louers, exhorting one another to be constant.

To the tune of Kypascie.

He famous Prince of *Macedon*,
whose wars increst his worthy name
Triumphed not so, when he had won
By conquest great, immortall fame,
    As I reioice, reioice,
For thee, my choice, with heart and voice,
        Since thou art mine,
Whom, long to loue, the Gods assigne.

¶ The secret flames of this my loue,
The stars had wrought ere I was borne,
Whose sugred force my hart doth moue,
And eke my will so sure hath sworne.
    that Fortunes lore, no more.
though I therefore, did life abhor[r]e :
        Shall neuer make,
Forgetful dewes my heat to slake.

¶ If that I false my faith to thee,
   Or seeke to chaunge for any newe :
   If thoughts appeare so ill in me,
   If thou thy life shall iustly rew.
      Such kinde of woe, of woe :
   As friende or foe, might to me showe :
         Betide me than,
   Or wurse, if it may hap to man.

¶ Then let vs ioy in this our loue :
   In spite of Fortunes wrath, my deere :
   Twoo willes in one, as dooth behooue,
   One loue in both, let still appeare :
      And I will be, will be,
   Piramus to thee, my owne *Thisbie,*
         So thou againe,
   My constant louer shalt remaine.

*A proper new Dity: Intituled Fie vpon Loue
and al his lawes.   To the tune of lumber me.*

Vch bitter fruict thy loue doth yeelde,
Such broken sleepes, such hope vnsure,
Thy call so oft hath me beguilde.
That I vnneth can well indure :
   But crie (alas) as I haue cause,
   Fie vpon Loue and all his Lawes.

¶ Like *Piramus,* I sigh and grone,
   VVhom Stonie wals, keept from his loue,
   And as the wofull *Palemon,*
   A thousand stormes, for thee I prooue,
      Yet thou a cruell Tigers whelpe,
      All slaiest the hart, whom thou maist help.

¶ A craggie Rocke, thy Cradle, was,
   And Tigers milke sure was thy foode,
   VVherby Dame Nature broought to passe,
   That like the Nurse should be thy moode :
      VVild and vnkinde, cruell and fell,
      to rent the hart that loues thee well.

¶ The Crocadile with fained teares,
The Fisher not so oft beguiles :
As thou hast luld my simple eares,
To here sweet words full fraught with wiles,
    that I may say, as I do prooue,
    VVo worth the time, I gan to loue.

¶ Sith thou hast vowd to worke my wrack
And hast no will my wealth to way :
Farewell vnkinde, I will keepe backe,
Such toyes as may my helth decay :
    and still will cry as I haue cause.
    Fie vpon Loue and all his lawes.

The Louer being wounded with his Ladis beutie, requireth mercy.

To the tune of Apelles.

He liuelie sparkes of those two eyes,
my wounded hart hath set on fire :
And since I can no way deuise,
To stay the rage of my desire,
    with sighs and trembling tears I craue
    my deare on me some pitie haue.

¶ In vewing thee, I tooke such ioy,
As one that sought his quiet rest :
Vntill I felt the fethered boy,
Ay flickring in my captiue brest :
    Since that time loe, in deepe dispaire,
    all voide of ioy, my time I weare.

¶ The wofull prisoner *Palemon.*
And *Troylus* eke kinge *Pyramus* sonne,
Constrained by loue did neuer mone :
As I my deer for thee haue done.
    Let pitie then requite my paines,
    My life and death in thee remaines.

¶ If constant loue may reape his hire,
And faith vnfained may purchace :
Great hope I haue to my desire.
Your gentle hart wil grant me grace,
 Til then (my deer) in few words plaine,
 In pensiue thoughts I shall remaine.

The lamentation of a woman being wrongfully
defamed. To the tune of Damon and Pithias.

Ou Ladies falsly deemd,
 of anie fault or crime :
Command your pensiue harts to help
 this dolefull tune of mine :
For spitefull men there are,
 that faults would fain espie :
Alas, what heart would heare their talke,
 but willingly would die.

¶ I waile oft times in woe,
 and curse mine houre of birth,
Such slanderous pangs do me oppresse,
 when others ioy in mirth :
Belike it was ordaind to be my destinie.
Alas what heart would heare their talk, &c.

¶ A thousand good women,
 haue guiltlesse been accusde :
For verie spite, although that they,
 their bodies neuer abusde :
the godly *Susanna* accusde was falsly
 alas &c.

¶ The poisoned *Pancalier*,
 ful falsly did accuse
The good Dutchesse of *Sauoy*,
 because she did refuse.
To grant vnto his loue,
 that was so vngodlie.
 Alas what, &c.

¶ Such false dissembling men,
    stoong with *Alectos* dart :
Must needs haue place to spit their spite,
    vpon some guiltlesse hart :
Therefore, I must be pleasde,
    that they triumph on me,
        Alas, &c.

¶ Therefore, Lord, I thee pray,
    the like death downe to send,
Vpon these false suspected men,
    or else their minds t'amend :
As thou hast done tofore,
    vnto these persons three.
        Alas what, &c.

A proper Song, Intituled : Fain wold I haue a pretie thing to giue vnto my Ladie.

To the tune of lustie Gallant.

¶ *Fain would I haue a pretie thing,*
    to giue vnto my Ladie :
I name no thing, nor I meane no thing,
    But as pretie a thing as may bee.

Wentie iorneyes would I make,
    and twentie waies would hie me,
To make aduenture for her sake,
    to set some matter by me :
But I would faine haue a pretie thing, &c,
I name nothing, nor I meane nothing, &c.

¶ Some do long for pretie knackes,
    and some for straunge deuices :
God send me that my Ladie lackes,
    I care not what the price is,
        thus faine, &c

¶ Some goe here, and some goe there,
    wheare gases be not geason :
And I goe gaping euery where,
    but still come out of season.
        Yet faine, &c.

¶ I walke the towne, and tread the streete,
    in euery corner seeking :
The pretie thinge I cannot meete,
    thats for my Ladies liking.
        Faine, &c.

¶ The Mercers pull me going by,
    the Silkie wiues say, what lacke ye ?
The thing you haue not, then say I,
    ye foolish fooles, go packe ye.
        But fain &c.

¶ It is not all the Silke in Cheape,
    nor all the golden treasure :
Nor twentie Bushels on a heape,
    can do my Ladie pleasure.
        But faine, &c.

¶ The Grauers of the golden showes,
    with Iuelles do beset me.
The Shemsters in the shoppes that sowes,
    they do nothing but let me :
        But faine, &c.

¶ But were it in the wit of man,
    by any meanes to make it,
I could for Money buy it than,
    and say, faire Lady, take it.
        Thus, fain, &c.

¶ O Lady, what a lucke is this :
    that my good willing misseth :
To finde what pretie thing it is,
    That my good Lady wisheth.

Thus fain wold I haue had this preti thing
 to giue vnto my Ladie :
I said no harme, nor I ment no harme,
 but as pretie a thing as may be.

A proper wooing Song, intituled : Maide
will ye loue me : ye or no ?

To the tune of the Mirchaunts Daughter
went ouer the fielde.

Ayde will ye loue me yea or no ?
tell me the trothe, and let me goe.
It can be no lesse then a sinfull deed,
 trust me truely,
To linger a Louer that lookes to speede.
 in due time duely.

¶ You Maids that thinke your selu[e]s as fine,
 As *Venus* and all the Muses nine :
The Father himselfe, when he first made man
 trust me truely :
Made you for his help when the world began
 in due time duely.

¶ Then sith Gods wil was euen so.
 Why should you disdaine you Louer tho ?
But rather with a willing heart,
 Loue him truely ?
For in so doing, you do but your. part,
 Let reason rule ye.

¶ Consider (sweet) what sighs and sobbes,
 Do nip my heart with cruell throbbes,
And al (my deer) for the loue of you,
 Trust me truly :
But I hope that you wil some mercie show,
 In due time duely.

¶ If that you do my case well way,
   And shew some signe whereby I may
   Haue some good hope of your good grace,
      Trust me truely :
   I count my selfe in a blessed case,
      Let reason rule ye.

¶ And for my part, whilst I do liue,
   To loue you most faithfully, my hand I giue,
   Forsaking all other, for your sweet sake,
      Trust me truly :
   In token whereof, my troth I betake,
      to your selfe most duely.

¶ And though for this time we must depart,
   yet keep you this ring tru[e] token of my hart,
   Til time do serue, we meet againe,
      Let reason rule ye.
   When an answer of comfort, I trust to obtain,
      In due time duly.

¶ Now must I depart with sighing teares,
   With sobbing heart and burning eares :
   Pale in the face, and faint as I may,
      trust me truly :
   But I hope our next meeting, a ioyfull day,
      in due time duly.

The painefull plight of a Louer oppressed
with the beautifull looks of his Lady.

To the tune of, I loued her ouer wel.

Hen as thy eies, ye wretched spies
   did breed my cause of care :
And sisters three did full agree,
   my fatall threed to spare.
      Then let these words ingrauen be,
         on toomb whereas I lie,
      That here lies one whom spiteful loue,
         hath caused for to die.

¶ Somtimes I spend the night to end,
  in dolors and in woe :
Somtime againe vnto my pain,
  my chiefest ioy doth grow.
      When as in minde, thy shape I finde,
        as fancie doth me tell :
      Whome now I knowe, as proofe doth show
        I loued thee ouer wel.

¶ How oft within my wreathed arme,
  desired I to folde :
Thy Christall corps, of whom I ioyed,
  more dearer than of golde.
      But now disdaine, dooth breede my paine,
        and thou canst not denie :
      But that I loued thee ouer well :
        that caused me die.

[¶] The hound that serues his Maisters will,
  in raunging here and there,
The moyling Horse, that labours still,
  his burthen great to beare :
      In lew of paine, receiues againe,
        of him which did him owe :
      As Natures heast, wiles most and least
        them thankefull for to showe.

¶ The Lyon and the Tyger fierce,
  as Nature doth them binde :
For loue, like loue repay againe :
  in Stories we doo finde :
      Those beasts and birds both wild and tame,
        of frendships lore can tell :
      But thy reply, willes me to die.
        that loued thee ouer well.

¶ Therfore, my deare and Darling faire,
  ensample take by those,
Which equally with loue againe,
  their louing mindes dispose :

And giue him glee, whose death we s[ee]
    approcheth very nie:
Without he gaine, to ease his paine,
    which loued thee hartely.

¶ Then shall th[e]y say that see the same,
    where euer that they goe :
And wish for ay, as for thy pay,
    all *Nestors* yeares to know :
      And I no lesse then all the rest,
        should wish thee health for aye :
      Because thou hast heard my request,
        and saued me from decay.

A faithfull vow of two constant Louers

To the new Rogero.

Hall distance part our loue,
    or daily choice of chaunge ?
Or sprites below, or Gods aboue,
    haue power to make vs straunge :

¶ No nothing here on earth,
    that kinde hath made or wrought,
Shall force me to forget.
    goodwill so dearely bought,

¶ And for any part I vow,
    to serue for terme of life :
Which promise may compare with her,
    which was *Vlisses* wife.

¶ Which vow if I doo breake,
    let vengeance on me fall,
Eche plague that on the earth may raigne,
    I aske not one, but all.

¶ Though time may breede suspect,
    to fill your hart with toyes ;
And absence may a mischefe breede,
    to let your wished ioyes :

¶ Yet thinke I haue a troth,
  and honesty to keepe:
And weigh the time your loue hath dwelt,
  within my hart so deep.

¶ And peise the words I spake,
  and marke my countenance then :
And let not slip no ernest sigh,
  if thou remember can.

¶ At least forget no teares,
  that trickled downe my face :
And marke howe oft I wroong your hand,
  and blushed all the space.

¶ Remember how I sware,
  and strook therewith my brest :
In witnesse when thou partst me fro,
  my heart with thee should rest.

¶ Thinke on the eger lookes,
  full loth to leaue thy sight,
That made the signes when that she list,
  to like no other wight.

¶ If this be out of thought,
  yet call to minde againe,
The busie sute, the much adoe,
  the labour and the paine,

¶ That at the first I had,
  ere thy good will I gate ;
And think how for thy loue alone,
  I purchase partly hate.

¶ But all is one with me,
  my heart so setled is :
No friend, nor foe, nor want of wealth,
  shall neuer hurt in this.

¶ Be constant now therefore,
    and faithfull to the end?
Be carefull how we both may do,
    to be ech others friend.

¶ With free and cleane consent,
    two hearts in one I knit :
Which for my part, I vow to keep,
    and promise not to flit,

¶ Now let this vow be kept,
    exchange thy heart for mine :
So shal two harts be in one breast,
    and both of them be thine.

A sorrowfull Sonet, made by M. George
Mannington, at Cambridge Castle.

To the tune of Labandala Shot.

Waile in wo, I plunge in pain,
with sorowing sobs, I do complain,
With wallowing waues I wish to die,
I languish sore whereas I lie,
    In feare I faint in hope I holde,
    With ruthe I runne, I was too bolde :
As lucklesse lot assigned me,
in dangerous dale of destinie :
    Hope bids me smile, Feare bids me weep,
    My seelie soule thus Care doth keep.

¶ Yea too too late I do repent,
    the youthful yeares that I haue spent,
The retch lesse race of carelesse kinde,
which hath betwitcht my woful minde.
    Such is the chaunce, such is the state,
    Of those that trust too much to fate.
No bragging boast of gentle blood,
What so he be, can do thee good :
    No wit, no strength, nor beauties hue,
    No friendly sute can death eschue.

¶ The dismall day hath had his wil,
And iustice seekes my life to spill :
Reuengement craues by rigorous law,
Whereof I little stood in awe :
 The dolefull doom to end my life,
 Bedect with care and worldlie strife :
And frowning iudge hath giuen his doome.
O gentle death thou art welcome :
 The losse of life, I do not feare,
 Then welcome death, the end of care.

¶ O prisoners poore, in dungeon deep,
Which passe the night in slumbring sleep :
Wel may you rue your youthful race.
And now lament your cursed cace.
 Content your selfe with your estate,
 Impute no shame to fickle fate :
With wrong attempts, increase no wealth,
Regard the state of prosperous health :
 And think on me, when I am dead :
 Whom such delights haue lewdly led.

¶ My friend and parents, where euer you be
Full little do you thinke on me :
My mother milde, and dame so deer :
Thy louing childe, is fettred heer :
 Would God I had, I wish too late,
 Been bred and borne of meaner estate :
Or else, would God my rechlesse eare,
Had been obedient for to heare,
 Your sage aduice and counsel true :
 But in the Lord parents adue.

¶ You valiant hearts of youthfull train,
Which heard my heauie heart complain :
A good example take by me,
Which runne the race where euer you be :
 trust not too much to bilbow blade,
 nor yet to fortunes fickle trade.

Hoist not your sailes no more in winde,
Least that some rocke, you chaunce to finde,
  or else be driuen to *Lybia* land,
  whereas the Barque may sinck in sand.

¶ You students all that present be,
To view my fatall destinie,
would God I could requite your pain,
wherein you labour, although in vain,
  if mightie God would think it good,
  to spare my life and vitall blood,
For this your profered curtesie,
I would remaine most stedfastly,
  Your seruant true in deed and word,
  But welcome death as please the Lord.

¶ Yea welcome death, the end of woe,
And farewell life, my fatall foe :
Yea welcome death, the end of strife,
Adue the care of mortall life,
  For though this life doth fleet away,
  In heauen I hope to liue for ay :
A place of ioy and perfect rest,
Which Christ hath purchaste for the best :
  Til that we meet in heauen most hiest :
  Adue, farewell in Iesu Christ.

*A proper Sonet, of an vnkinde Damsell, to
to her faithful Louer. To, the nine Muses.*

He ofter that I view and see,
That plesant face and faire beautie,
  whereto my heart is bound :
The neer my Mistresse is to me,
My health is farthest off I see :
  and fresher is my wound :
Like as the flame doth quench by fire,
  or streams consume by raigne,
So doth the sight that I desire,
  appease my grief and paine :

Like a flie that doth hie,
   and haste into the fire :
So in brief, findes her grief,
   that thought to sport aspire.

¶ When first I saw those Christal streams,
   I little thought on beauties beams :
     sweet venom to haue found,
But wilful wil did prick me foorth,
Perforce to take my grief in woorth,
     that causd my mortall wound :
And *Cupid* blind compeld me so,
     my fruitlesse hope to hide :
Wherein remaind my bitter wo :
     thus stil he did me guide ?
Then his dart, to my hart,
   he slung with cruell fist :
Whose poison fel, I know right wel,
   no louer may resist.

¶ Thus vainly stil, I frame my sute,
Of ill sowen seeds, such is the frute,
     experience doth it show :
The fault is hers the pain is mine,
And thus my sentence I define,
     I hapned on a shrow :
And now beware, ye yongmen all,
     Example take by mee :
Least beauties bait in *Cupids* thrall,
     do catch you priuily :
So stay you, I pray you,
   and marke you my great wrong,
Forsaken, not taken,
   thus end I now my song.

The Louer complaineth the absence of his Ladie, wisheth for death.

To, the new Almaine.

Ith spitefull spite hath spide her time,
 my wished ioies to end :
And drowping dread hath driuen me now
 from my new chosen friend :
 I can but waile the want,
 of this my former ioie :
Sith spiteful force hath sought so long,
 my blisse for to annoie.

¶ But though it be our chance
 asunder for to be,
My heart in pawne til we do meet,
 Shal stil remaine with thee :
 And then we shall renue,
 our sugred pleasures past :
And loue that loue, that seekes no change,
 whilst life in vs do last.

¶ Perhaps my absence may,
 or else some other let :
By choice of change, cause thee my deer,
 our former loue forget :
 And thou renounce the oth,
 which erst thou vowdst to me :
My deerest blood in recompence,
 thou sure shouldst shortly see.

[¶] A thousand sighs to send to thee I wil not let,
Ne to bewaile the losse of thee, I neuer will forget
 But still suppose I see,
 the same before my face :
And louingly between my armes,
 thy corps I do embrace.

¶ Thus feed I fancie stil,
    for lacke of greater ioy :
With such like thoughts, which daily doth,
    my wofull heart annoy :
    thus stil in hope I liue,
        my wished ioies to haue :
And in dispaire oft time I wish,
    my feeble Corps in graue.

¶ This is the life I leade, til I thee see again
And so wil do, til dreadful death,
    do seek to ease my paine,
whom rather I do wish, by force to end in wo,
than for to liue in happie state,
    thy loue for to forgo.

¶ And thus farewell my deer,
    with whom my heart shall rest,
Remember him that this did write,
    sith he doth loue thee best :
And wil til greedie death,
    my daies do shorten now :
Farewel my dear, loe here my faith
    and troth to thee I vow.

Finis.

The Louer compareth him self to the pain-
ful Falconer. *To the tune, I loued her ouer wel.*

THe soaring hawk from fist that flies,
    her Falconer doth constraine :
Sometime to range the ground vnknown,
    to find her out againe :
And if by sight or sound of bell,
    his falcon he may see :
wo ho he cries, with cheerful voice,
    the gladdest man is he.

¶ By Lure then in finest sort,
   he seekes to bring her in :
But if that she, ful gorged be,
   he can not so her win :
Although her becks and bending eies,
   she manie proffers makes :
Wo ho ho he cries, awaie she flies,
   and so her leaue she takes.

¶ This wofull man with wearie limmes,
   runnes wandring round about :
At length by noise of chattering Pies,
   his hawke againe found out
His heart was glad his eies had seen,
   his falcon swift of flight :
Wo ho ho he cries, she emptie gorgde,
   vpon his Lure doth light.

¶ How glad was then the falconer there,
   no pen nor tongue can tel :
He swam in blisse that lately felt
   like paines of cruel hel.
His hand somtime vpon her train,
   somtime vpon her brest :
Wo ho ho he cries with chearfull voice,
   his heart was now at rest.

¶ My deer likewise, beholde thy loue,
   what paines he doth indure :
And now at length let pitie moue,
   to stoup vnto his Lure.
A hood of silk, and siluer belles,
   new gifts I promise thee :
Wo ho ho, I crie, I come then saie,
   make me as glad as hee.

FINIS.